Apricot Jam

A short story
by
Prudence Webster

ISBN-13: 978-1-911-24905-4

The fit is momentary; upon a thought
He will again be well.

Shakespeare

Apricot Jam

FOUR TALL STONE statues. They stood on the horizon. More precisely, they stood on the playground, which fell *just* a few millimetres short of the real horizon line.

Cate was judging that very distance through squinting eyes as she stood by the apartment window wondering why she had not seen the statues before. They were massive. Too much to take in really. Like Blue Whales and Stealth Bombers.

Their speckled granite mass, deep and warm it seemed from where she was, must be exhaustingly heavy.

It was the heaviness that bothered her. Why had she not heard them arrive? And how could they be moved away? The roads and buildings around would have shaken when the stone giants appeared. Juddering would have interrupted everyone during days of granite planting. So, contrary to her instincts about them, these statues must have crept up during the night, all unseen. Unseen until they shone there now for the first time. Exuding weight.

They were almost centred in her window frame, which added narrative and impact, heightening her sense of their having been placed there for her. Ideally (and this was already on her mind, nagging away at her equilibrium) the window frame did need pushing out a little to the left if a balanced composition was to be achieved. She might try to do this after her breakfast. She stepped a little to her right as a makeshift compromise, almost without realising, but this new position at once felt contrived and she shifted back self-consciously.

She turned as she heard Rob yawning. He emerged from their bedroom, heralded by dynamic deodorant fumes that claimed no antiperspirant powers because sweating was a good thing babe, as long as it was fragrant. It was a long time since she'd seen him sweat actually.

"Look, out there …" she said pointing, as he picked up his big flipchart.

"Yeah, see you later babe. Let me know what you're gonna cook tonight – text me." And Rob, taking with him his charisma and coloured permanent markers, was gone.

He had first noticed Cate three years ago in the pub at the bottom of his road. She'd had oversized gold hooped earrings in and that, together with the length and shade of her hair, had reminded him of a neighbour he'd been infatuated with the year before. She definitely had a specific girl-next-door look. He'd made his move almost straightaway.

She'd been normal when he met her. He was sure she had. She was a graduate for shit's sake! She must have had something about her. He thought of himself as a bit of a loser made good. A kosher intellectual on his arm would augment his kudos and tall intelligent women had always turned him on: he'd just never managed to engage one.

He recalled their first date. Letting her climb the restaurant stairs in front of him had no doubt been interpreted as a chivalrous gesture, but he'd only wanted to get a good view of her size ten dress working its way step by step to the top. Not enough stairs! Not enough stairs! Good grief.

They'd sat down and he'd tried to guess her age. Twenty? Nineteen? Eighteen? Bloody hell. He'd started to sweat, a good thing. He was twenty-seven.

Seventeen? She'd
laughed. 'Twenty-two!'

And then she'd looked concerned that he might be disappointed! Not at all, he'd thought. As taut and fresh as a seventeen year old girlfriend would be, the angst would have tainted the pleasure. No, she was perfect.

4

Did Cate still look young for her age, he wondered? He couldn't tell. In all honesty – he pulled on the handbrake particularly aggressively as he parked and realised – he didn't care.

The statues were still there, Cate was sure of it. Everything seemed pin sharp this morning.

As she dressed, away from the window, she pictured them. They were already haunting her. The tallest man in the middle, profiled, challenging her. Two other stone men stood, with less height, but still tall and strong. Then, on the right as she had looked, a horse or pony it seemed to be, with blinkered eyes and a sad aspect, completed the strange tableau.

Dressed now, she deliberately didn't look out there again. Negative suggestion made this difficult of course and at one point she focused on the middle distance to watch the statues indirectly, in the manner that soldiers are taught to regard compasses and watches in the dark. These glimpses suggested to her that the stone horse had started to rock slowly, backwards and forwards. Noiselessly and with sadness. It was sinister. A rocking horse, from nowhere. Its soundless slow rocking filled the silence in a sickening way. A spongy emptiness or absence that recurred every couple of seconds, in the space in front of it and then in the space behind.

Suddenly, and it really was very sudden this, she had an overwhelming desire to cover the statues, all of them, in sticky apricot jam. She imagined the treacle-like substance slowly inching down the statues in syrupy rivulets that covered everything. Pale orange magma that clung and suffocated rather than burned. It became more than a vision. It became something she had to realise.

The difficulty would be managing a bucket big enough and a ladder tall enough. Neither was she very strong, or good with heights.

There was no need for Rob to call into the office at nine. His presentation, seventy miles away, could have been his first stop and allowed him a lie-in. But he wanted to see his colleagues. He wanted to see

Charlie, specifically.

Charlie wasn't boring or tired. Charlie didn't burst into tears when he looked at her. When he talked Charlie had spontaneous answers. Sport was her thing so she was always tanned and full of energy: she'd been Buck's heptathlon champion two years running. How impressive would that sound when he eventually introduced her down the pub?

He asked her if she was up for one of their 'quick meets' at The Plough around three. So far these had only involved intense flirting, but he'd booked a room at the nearby Holiday Inn in the hope that, this afternoon, she'd agree a room was what she'd been wanting too.

He sweated a little. She had agreed to the Plough entreé. Slight mistake this morning, he thought: asking Cate to plan food. He now had to let her know that he'd be late home but would grab something while he was out. Not that it was like Cate to give much thought to food lately. He couldn't imagine that Charlie would ever buy processed food, or 'ready meals for two'. If she had a burger, he was sure she'd follow it with a homemade fruit smoothie or shot of wheatgrass.

He needed that: something exotic. Something life-giving.
He wanted to feel his blood circulate again.

As irony would have it, Cate was in a supermarket when she got his no-food-needed-tonight-babe message: she was buying apricot jam. At the till, her basket was loaded high with enough jam jars to fill a bucket. She was warned against bulk buying however, and only twelve got scanned. More trips to different shops were called for and it was past midday by the time she got back with the amount she probably needed.

After the first thirty jars or so, it was clear that there would not be enough jam to fill the bucket and so Cate started to add water as she went along. She was pleased that this had the double-effect of thinning the conserve, that had been disappointingly gelatinous and almost solid, and of rendering paler the overall shade of orange.

It was a golden fruit treacle now, just right. She was invincible. She felt a rush.

She felt so successful that for a moment there was an element of clarity to her thoughts and she realised that she wouldn't be able to carry a tall ladder *with* her heavy bucket all the way across the roads, to the park just in front of the horizon.

But she felt equally strongly that she would find a tall ladder on the way or that, if not, a swing or a roundabout would be close by to give her a leg-up on one of the statues.

Too scared, she hadn't looked at the stone statues since the morning. In fact she'd only seen them clearly that once. The fear she entertained was a thrilling fear, akin to when you know someone is there watching you, but you scream anyway when you dare to look back at them. Or when you know that Glenn Close isn't really dead, but you jump when she splashes out of the bath. Cate had pulled down the blinds hours ago to avoid that adrenalin.

Strange, how no one passed her on her way to the statues that dark cold evening at six o'clock. Maybe people did see her. Perhaps she walked right past someone on her way down the steps from her apartment. She didn't notice them, or hear them if they tried to speak to her or ask what was in her bucket. She was on a mission and this was going to be a perfect moment.

She had stood in front of the mirror by the door for at least an hour before picking up the bucket and leaving. She had wanted to be sure that her hair was just right. Her long coat had been buttoned, unbuttoned, and buttoned again before she had left it open. Sweet culinary efforts had given her face a natural glow. Her eyes were shining and she flickered a smile at her reflection. But her hair really did have to be right. She pinned it up again, very precisely.

As she crossed the road with her coat flying she felt the freshness of the evening on her. A sensation of healthy cold that she had felt in the past and since forgotten. She was aware that her coat was waving out behind her as she leant forward into the evening wind. A pin came loose from her hair and she could feel the stray strands waving now too.

She knew that the wind, pressing as it did against her blouse, was outlining the underneath of her breasts and that it was pushing down flat against her stomach.

She guessed that she looked like an impeccable Kate Winslett on the prow of the 'Titanic'. She fancied herself as a new character from the surreal novel 'Mr Weston's Good Wine', very sharply-drawn. This was her 'Good Jam'.

Her bare feet felt the prickly edge of the park's grass so she looked up. All she could see was a roundabout, a twisted slide, and some swings. A huddle of teenagers stood laughing at her and the bucket. She couldn't see her statues.

What had happened? The cold dark was real. Her feet were frozen. She looked a mess: she knew. She felt some unruly hairpins like frozen cobwebs blowing against her throat. Traffic reached her ears along with music and voices. Teenagers were using their phones. Maybe taking pictures, maybe kinder ones were calling the police.

Rob derived some sort of pleasure from driving to his booked room via his home address. There was no risk attached to it, no additional increase in heart rate. He just liked the mild peril. He did slow down a little when he saw the blue flashing light in the park but, at the end of the day babe, his mind was already full.

Poetry

Misfit

It seems right in our post-brillo-box-world
that Nana walked four miles daily for bread -
her black fur hat against the cold Welsh rain
Cockney legs bowed (but we said bandy) and
a brown leather bag with swinging buckles -
to avoid the shop with no packaging.

Sweep a bird's eye view across her landscape,
ancient and aching with hill-drenched being.
Note the tin roof of the shed-like building,
the old *siop* she might have gone in.
Bread it had, piles of it, punching out fistfuls of warm doughy air
and a cat accepting its warmth as his.

Fur dripped between the gaps in the loaves
with the heaviness of his purring body –
coat of gloss oozed down a crumbling wall.
Nothing to dissuade him he sat on them all.
He liked his bread fresh and warm from the baker.
Cat on a split tin loaf.

So it was that a glance at the grocer
blowing fur from a yeasty purchase
made her walk into town for our bread.

1976

Mrs Jackson frowns: "you're looking for a
needle in a haystack".
She with flesh folded old arms and those
bold chiascuro permanent curls.

Unmoved caretaker's wife. The vast acres
of brown parched playing field elaborate
the smarting space
of my small earlobe's bare expanse.

Mown grass, evening, wavering light she
unlocks the gate and I scan
that field: Ted Hughes' Iron Man. Other
ear sends out bright signals.

Small foot kicks roughly piles of grass. I
leave in tears, half-hearted.
There's wisdom in old sayings but
I hate her old age, holding the key.

Kitchen Sink Drama

When done she takes her yoghurt pot, not washed, and fills it brim-full with whatever leftovers are lying around. Potato peelings take up a lot of space but are often present. The dirt they are coated with when organic can tarnish her nails and define her finger prints as they are pushed down the pot to make more room. Dull juice sponges out but can be tipped away - though this doesn't really help the volume - though it should? The pile of peelings scraped across the worktop with a Michelin flourish is slow to diminish and the pot fills quickly. Her heart beat increases as the task becomes ridiculous and the pushing and draining reaches dizzy heights of ambition. Even when the pot is full the longer peelings can be draped across if she finds their centres of gravity and this will still count. Her index finger is the pivot point as she carries the bloated and garnished pot to the bin which is a carrier bag on the kitchen door handle. If the pot splits another peeling or two might be wedged in through the side, it is not cheating, especially as the mission
 is   never
successful.

Titanoboa Lutonensis

'A forty two foot
[Fossil] snake would squeeze
But barely through a
Normal size door.'

I suck in my cheeks

And clench my muscles
So sensing myself

Suddenly slim

'Ain't she powerful?'
The scientist says
With a nervous laugh.

Ha yeah. Not half.

Goat

I found a goat in my cupboard
today he was sitting next to
jam pots and packets of rice. He
looked out at me and his eyes told
me that he'd been there since a kid,
I'd just forgotten him - truly
I had. I felt awful, no joke,
so I tapped a shoulder three times.
Incredibly he knew to jump.
Somehow then I knew him too, his
legs encircled me, I loved him
lightly and happily with my
entire being. I was meant to
care deep for him - this made me feel
worse. From the hard white grey bristles
of his mandibles to hidden
moist pink gums that rubbed on my cheek
it was like coming home, goodness
knows how he must have felt before
with dark jars and printed cardboard.

Nothing had been eaten I'd have
noticed so I showed him the lawn
from shoulder height and gentle set him
down, in the sun that warmed him through.
I went mad pulling out carrots
and spring onions and I lined them

so neatly in appetising
rows, vegetable regiments,
they looked good and the grass was bright.
And I pulled out more to show how
much he meant and the lines went on
so that the red earth gaped and groaned
and it was all good - then he ate.
Not what I gave but what he found
himself with his nose and hooves from
the same dug soil where he settled.
Leaves hung from his moving lips
his eyes set into knowing gold
white elbows, shoulders owned the space.
I left him there knowing he'd stay.

Gift Shower

I saw as I left the house
that my cat left her night-time's trophies
outside our door. (– Scapula tense
still held rigid as in mid run)
a dead middle-sized rat
and a cast-off finch's nest.

Afternoon, "the heavens opened".
Then I saw them sodden still side by
side on the blackening stone steps.
The rain was relentless: and for
seconds at least two of us
looked like drowned rats. We needed cover.

The wet nest stretched elastically.
Its knitted moss lent an oval
That held the tip of the rat's tail, feet, ears, nose, egg-shaped.
Snug as a mouse in a tea cosy,
Rasta rat in primitive colours.
Brown beanie coffin.

Snowdrops

weight's a true metaphor for grief.

so when I planted snowdrops there
on the freshly tiled turf and
they did not grow I knew just why:

when all my heavy fallen tears
sink down, in a ground of crowded
thoughts, and the heave of hurt, that
hovers
above the blades of fresh cut grass,

weighs too and presses;
buds grow downwards only, to be
there with her.

one day that space might hold too much;
maybe then some flowers will show.

Death in the Wings

Path-fallen she lies twitching quietly
feathered costume clings to her beating
breast: staying hot, channelling oxygen,
quickly, through urgent, leaking red.

The dog runs only to the Prima Dove
performing death with heartfelt thud
hitting the waving field's mise en scène,
game for a laugh, with decorum.

www.ingramcontent.com/pod-product-compliance
Lightning Source LLC
Chambersburg PA
CBHW071230130626
46555CB00004B/1922